Head, Shoulders, Knees and Toes

Cabeza, hombros, rodillas y dedos

WRITTEN BY • ESCRITO POR
Skye Silver

ILLUSTRATED BY • ILUSTRADO POR
Mariana Ruiz Johnson

TRANSLATED BY • TRADUCIDO POR
María A. Pérez

Barefoot Books
step inside a story

Head, shoulders, knees and toes! Head, shoulders, knees and toes!
Eyes and ears and mouth and nose —
This is how your body grows.

¡Cabeza, hombros, rodillas y dedos!
¡Cabeza, hombros, rodillas y dedos!
Ojos y orejas y boca y nariz . . .
Así es como tu cuerpo crece.

Let's get a healthy start today.
Fresh and clean, that's the way!

Empecemos de forma saludable hoy.
Frescos y limpios, ¡así es!

Wash your hands and shake them dry.
Shake them low and shake them high.
Let's all shake them! Don't be shy.
Shake them low and shake them high!

Lávate las manos y sacúdelas para secarlas.
Sacúdelas hacia abajo y sacúdelas hacia arriba.
¡Vamos a sacudirlas! No seas tímido.
¡Sacúdelas hacia abajo y sacúdelas hacia arriba!

Let's find something good to eat.
Yummy food, oh, what a treat!

Vamos a buscar algo bueno que comer.
Comida sabrosa, oh, ¡qué delicia!

Humming with a happy hum,
Rub your tummy and say "Yum!"
Crunching, munching every crumb,
Rub your tummy and say "Yum!"

Tarareando con un tarareo feliz,
frótate la barriguita y di: "¡Rico!".
Masticando y saboreando cada migaja,
frótate la barriguita y di: "¡Rico!".

On our way to school, we like to share.
Kindness shows our friends we care.

De camino a la escuela, nos gusta compartir.
La bondad indica a nuestros amigos que nos importan.

When your school friends all arrive,
Give each one a big high-five.
Sharing kindness, smiling wide,
Give your friends a big high-five!

Cuando lleguen tus amigos de la escuela,
choca esos cinco con cada uno.
Comparte bondad, con una gran sonrisa,
¡choca esos cinco con tus amigos!

We all love to play outside!
Jump, shout, stretch and slide.

¡Nos encanta jugar afuera!
Salta, grita, estírate y deslízate.

Reaching up and reaching down,
Turn your body all around.
Can you touch your fingers to the ground?
Turn your body all around!

Levanta los brazos y bájalos,
gira el cuerpo a la redonda.
¿Puedes tocar el piso con los dedos?
¡Gira el cuerpo a la redonda!

It's storytime — just what we need!
Choose a picture book to read.

Es la hora del cuento . . .
¡justo lo que nos hace falta!
Escoge un libro ilustrado para leer.

Gather round the story rug.
Give your listening ears a tug.
All together feeling snug,
Give your listening ears a tug!

Júntense en la alfombra de los cuentos.
Dense un tironcito de la oreja de escuchar.
Todos juntitos, muy cómodos.
¡Dense un tironcito de la oreja de escuchar!

Time to wind down from the day,
And take it easy after play.

Es hora de acabar el día.
Y de relajarse después del juego.

Let's curl up and get some sleep.
Breathe in slow and breathe in deep.
Let your breath out, soft and sweet.
Breathe in slow and breathe in deep.

Vamos a acurrucarnos y dormir.

Inhala despacio e inhala hondo.

Exhala suave y dulcemente.

Inhala despacio e inhala hondo.

Head, shoulders, knees and toes!
Head, shoulders, knees and toes!
Eyes and ears and mouth and nose —
This is how your body grows.

¡Cabeza, hombros, rodillas y dedos!
¡Cabeza, hombros, rodillas y dedos!
Ojos y orejas y boca y nariz . . .
Así es como tu cuerpo crece.

Healthy Habits for Your Growing Body!

¡Hábitos saludables para tu cuerpo en crecimiento!

Hygiene • Higiene

Did you know that germs, bacteria and viruses (things that make us sick) wind up on our bodies every day? Washing your hands after you use the toilet and before eating is one of the most important things you can do to keep yourself and those around you healthy.

Your turn! To make sure you're washing your hands long enough, sing the alphabet from A to Z while you wash. Then rinse and dry carefully.

¿Sabías que gérmenes, bacterias y virus (cosas que nos enferman) acaban en nuestro cuerpo diariamente? Lavarse las manos después de ir al baño y antes de comer es una de las cosas más importantes que puedes hacer para que, tanto tú como los que te rodean, estén sanos.

¡Te toca! Para estar seguro de lavarte bien las manos, canta el alfabeto de la A a la Z al lavártelas. Luego enjuágatelas y sécatelas con cuidado.

Healthy food • Comida saludable

Some foods are better for your body than others because they give your body more vitamins, minerals and protein — nutrients you need in order to move, breathe, keep warm, heal when you get sick and build strong bones. Including healthy foods like vegetables, fruits and whole grains in your diet will give you energy and help you feel your best!

Your turn! Try filling half your plate with bright fruits and vegetables. Can you eat a rainbow of foods?

Algunas comidas son mejores para el cuerpo que otras porque le dan más vitaminas, minerales y proteínas: nutrientes que necesitas para moverte, respirar, estar calentito, sanarte cuando te enfermas y tener huesos fuertes. Incluir comidas saludables como vegetales, frutas y granos enteros en tu dieta te dará energía y te ayudará a sentirte bien.

¡Te toca! Procura llenar la mitad de tu plato con frutas y vegetales coloridos. ¿Eres capaz de comer un arcoíris de alimentos?

Exercise • Ejercicio

When you stretch, run, play on the playground, participate in sports, dance or do any movement activity, you strengthen your bones and muscles and even lower your chances of getting certain diseases. Plus, exercise can help you sleep better and feel happier!

Your turn! Ask a grown-up to help you record how much time you spend doing physical activity one day. Any type of exercise or active play counts. Aim for 30 minutes or more!

Cuando te estiras, corres, juegas en el parque, participas en deportes, bailas o haces cualquier actividad que requiera movimiento, fortaleces los huesos y músculos, y hasta reduces las posibilidades de contraer ciertas enfermedades. Además, ¡el ejercicio te ayuda a dormir mejor y estar más feliz!

¡Te toca! Pídele a un adulto que te ayude a anotar el tiempo que pasas en actividades físicas durante un día. Cualquier tipo de ejercicio o de juego activo cuenta. ¡Procura que sean 30 minutos o más!

Kindness towards others • Bondad hacia los demás

Believe it or not, being kind to other people is good for our bodies! When you do kind things, your brain releases a chemical called serotonin that makes you feel happier and even makes your heart healthier. And, of course, kindness makes other people feel good too.

Your turn! Find something caring you can do every day! You could play with a child who seems lonely, comfort a friend who is sad or help your family with chores at home. There are so many ways to be kind to others.

Aunque no lo creas, ¡ser bondadoso es bueno para el cuerpo! Cuando realizas actos bondadosos, tu cerebro libera una sustancia química llamada serotonina que te hace sentir feliz y beneficia a tu corazón. Y, por supuesto, la bondad también hace sentir bien a los demás.

¡Te toca! ¡Busca algo bondadoso que puedas hacer diariamente! Podrías jugar con un niño que esté solo, consolar a un amigo que esté triste o ayudar a tu familia con los quehaceres. Hay muchas maneras de ser bondadosos con los demás.

Reading • Leer

Being healthy means taking care of our bodies and our minds. When you read or listen to stories, your memory gets a workout, which helps it grow stronger. Reading regularly also helps you learn new words and teaches your brain how to think about complicated ideas. Now that's smart!

Your turn! Even if you don't know how to read on your own, you can look at the pictures in books and tell your own stories. Visit the children's section of your local library to find a whole world of books to read!

Estar saludable conlleva cuidar del cuerpo y de la mente. Cuando lees o escuchas cuentos, tu memoria se entrena, y eso la fortalece. Leer a menudo también te ayuda a aprender nuevas palabras y le enseña a tu cerebro a pensar en ideas complejas. ¡Eso sí que es ser listo!

¡Te toca! Aunque no sepas leer por tu cuenta, puedes mirar las imágenes en los libros e inventarte tus propios cuentos. ¡Vete a la sección de libros infantiles de la biblioteca de tu zona para descubrir todo un mundo de libros que puedes leer!

Sleep • El sueño

Sleep gives our bodies a chance to rest and our brains a chance to sort out everything we've learned during the day. Getting enough sleep can help put you in a good mood and make you less likely to get sick.

Your turn! Make sure you get a good night's sleep! If you have trouble sleeping, you can try gentle stretching, deep breathing, reading or listening to a story to help your body rest.

El sueño hace que el cuerpo descanse y que el cerebro ponga en orden lo que hemos aprendido durante el día. Dormir lo suficiente te ayuda a estar de buen humor y hace que te enfermes menos.

¡Te toca! ¡Asegúrate de dormir bien por la noche! Si te cuesta dormir, intenta estirarte suavemente, respirar hondo, leer o escuchar un cuento para ayudar a tu cuerpo a descansar.

For Elias

Para Elias

— S. S.

To Pato, Pepo
and Felix, my family

Para Pato, Pepo y
Félix, mi familia.

— M. R. J.

Barefoot Books
23 Bradford Street, 2nd Floor
Concord, MA 01742

Text copyright © 2020 by Skye Silver. Illustrations copyright © 2020 by Mariana Ruiz Johnson
The moral rights of Skye Silver and Mariana Ruiz Johnson have been asserted

First published in the United States of America by Barefoot Books, Inc in 2020
This bilingual Spanish paperback edition first published in 2021

Graphic design by Sarah Soldano, Barefoot Books
Edited and art directed by Kate DePalma, Barefoot Books
Educational notes by Stefanie Paige Wieder, M.S.Ed., Child Development Expert
Translated by María A. Pérez
Reproduction by Bright Arts, Hong Kong
Printed in China
This book was typeset in Balsamiq Sans, Kidprint MT and PhoenixChunky
The illustrations were prepared in mixed media
combined with digital techniques

ISBN 978-1-64686-375-4

Library of Congress Cataloging-in-Publication
Data for the English edition is
available under LCCN 2020009322

5 7 9 8 6